GOLIATH AND I

GOLIATH AND I

GOLIATH AND I

Rashmi Kumar

2018

Goliath and I - published by the Rev. Dr. Ashish Amos of the Indian Society for Promoting Christian Knowledge (ISPCK), Post Box 1585, Kashmere Gate, Delhi-110006.

© Author, 2018

Online order: http://ispck.org.in/book.php

Also available on amazon.in

ISBN: 978-81-8465-686-2

Laser typeset by

ISPCK, Post Box 1585, 1654, Madarsa Road, Kashmere Gate, Delhi-110006 • *Tel:* 23866323

e-mail: ashish@ispck.org.in • ella@ispck.org.in
website: www.ispck.org.in

To,

Jesus.

**My friend. My father.
My confidante. My guide.**

I can't imagine any day without you.

Contents

Preface

Many would wonder why "Goliath and I?" Why couldn't it be Jesus and I, or Lord and I or the Holy Spirit and I or similar such spiritually-filled positive combos? Well, let me explain. Each one of us lives with our own Goliath. Sometimes, at our workplaces. At times, inside our homes. And several times, right within our hearts and minds.

Unfortunately, this giant is more predominant than Jesus is, for most of us. I for one, definitely fall into that category. Time and again, I have failed as a David. This shepherd boy in me has been all too weak to withstand Mr G. I have also lacked the simple techniques of a sling and stone to combat my enemy. I try to strategize. Make complex plans. Analyze paralyze… And what not! My David has been anything but confident in his walk with the Lord. He has lacked the courage and persistence to fight the fight that only and truly comes from having a galaxy-sized faith in the Lord.

Okay. So the next question. Why am I even writing this book then? And, I'm going to make a quick full sweep at answering that.

Five years ago I had no idea who David was. Yes, you heard it right. I HAD NO IDEA WHO DAVID WAS. I mean I knew him through David and Goliath kind of story situation. But that was it. And up until five years ago, I had no idea who Jesus was (don't let me cap this. Confessions take a lot of courage!) Again, I knew Him. But, more like I would know the cashier at my grocery store.

Then something dramatic happened and that was going to change my life forever. Five years ago, after I moved to Canada, my life started to nose dive.

I underwent acute isolation, cultural and social shift and a complete loss of my own identity. From being a super active person, who loved her job as a journalist and essentially thrived on fashion and travel, I coiled up to someone who I couldn't relate with anymore. I was always sensitive to shifts and changes in my life, but this was epic. This was totally something else! I had no idea that moving away from my home country would have such a deep negative impact on my well-being. Although, I had my little piece of heaven with me, as my son… But in this book I am not going to talk much about it. Days turned into months and months into years and each day I questioned God. "Why did He choose to dump me in one of the coldest countries in the world? Once a social butterfly, why wasn't I able to make

                                            PREFACE

new friends again? Why couldn't He just stop me when I was making plans to leave India? Like, do something dramatic… Something that would have never taken me away from home… Has He turned deaf to my problems? Was He even listening? Was He?"

And like all selfish humans, who turn to God only in desperation, I did the same. This time, my logical argument about the existence of God went flying out of the window… So far that it left no patch marks on the cottony snow of my January backyard!

The logic was replaced by a desperate need to be loved, understood, coached, and comforted and most of all, something that I could just cling on to. It didn't matter for how long! Thankfully, Jesus was strong enough to bear my weight (quite literally as I was 20 kilos up due to emotional eating) for way too long.

Today, as I write this, I pause to think about that time. If that time of nothingness had never happened to me, I'd have never known Jesus. And David. And Goliath. Not to say that what I had in India was bad. In fact, I know I'd carry memories from that country for a lifetime, but those memories had no place for Jesus. My mind can't process India-Jesus, but it can certainly correlate Canada-Jesus. Because this is where the shepherd boy in me finally decided to pick up his sling and stone with quivering hands. This is where I clung on to verses from the Bible as if they were my special meal for the day. Back then, I didn't know that every chapter I read and every prayer I said was miraculously taking me closer to God.

Through this book, I want to share those Bible verses that had the most impact at a time when I needed them the most. Some of these verses literally popped out to speak to me directly.

I would like you to be a part of this personal journey because this was the only time I realized that God was alive. And I want you to believe that… If a rational, analytically-brained person like me could.

1

Feeling sorry? Well, don't!

Jeremiah 15:15-21

When these verses first revealed to me through *Our Daily Bread* I had to read them repeatedly to understand what Lord wanted to tell me. So while the entire chapter is talking directly to prophet Jeremiah, I pretended that these seven verses were relevant to my situation. And isn't that how Bible should be applied to our personal lives anyway? Because as a matter of fact, something or the other was always spoken to someone or the other in the Bible, so how do you draw help from it? My open secret? I convince myself that whichever Bible verse I read has a reason to pop open in front of me when I need it the most, and of course, all this while placing a firm belief that Lord is speaking to ME directly.

So what caught my fancy was verse 18 and onwards, which says, "Why do I keep on suffering? Why are my wounds incurable? Why won't they heal? Do you intend to disappoint me like a stream that goes dry in the summer? (*Verse 18*). This verse precisely summarized how I felt. My pain of isolation and sense of displacement was so acute that it DID feel like a wound that would never cure itself. I had lost meaning to move with lack of professional and personal goals. However, there was a ready answer for me in verse 19, "If you return, I will take you back, and you will be my servant again. If instead of talking nonsense you proclaim a worthwhile message, you will be my prophet again. The people will come back to you, and you will not need to go to them."

Let's put the limelight on Jeremiah here for a moment. (Like me) this prophet is complaining to God about lack of motivation or pleasure in his work. God then calls the prophet to cease from his distrust, and to return to his work. By doing so, Jeremiah is given an assurance to be delivered from his enemies. To put it simply, those who are with God, and faithful to Him, will be delivered from trouble or given enough strength to carry through it. Many things appear frightful (like they did in my life), or your life or in Jeremiah's life, but sometimes all God wants us to do is to stop "talking nonsense," or feeling sorry for our situation and proclaim what is meaningful and positive and move on.

However, God's tough love is multidimensional. Through verses 20 and 21, He knows well to reassure and wouldn't you

     FEELING SORRY? WELL, DON'T!

agree that He does a great job of it? If these two concluding verses don't charge your adrenalin, I don't know what will! "I will make you like a solid bronze wall as far as they are concerned. They will fight against you, but they will not defeat you. I will be with you to protect you and keep you safe," (*Verse 20*). "I will rescue you from the power of wicked and violent people," (*Verse 21*).

2

When you're punished, you're loved

Hebrews 12:3-11

My first reaction to these nine verses was, "Like really? Okay, I don't want to be loved." I don't reprimand my four-year-old (mostly) even when he strongly believes that the entire house is a huge garbage bin and the remains of anything that he doesn't eat or is waste in his eyes, could simply be tossed around the house – why does then Lord deal with His own children so harshly sometimes? I mean, I am a human and I don't… But He is God, right?!

And, if there has ever been any struggle in your life, you'd know exactly what I am talking about. I am in no way suggesting that all problems in your or my life are a culmination of Christ's timeout sessions – if there is one truth

I have realized and that is – suffering and living go hand in hand. One cannot be devoid of the other. Yes, some have more and some less, but that again is subjective. Loading or unloading a dishwasher could be someone's biggest nightmare, while for another, not having hands to do this basic chore could make all the difference between life and death!

Anyway, I am done digressing enough, now back to Hebrews.

Somehow, it seemed unfair that the loved ones get all the brickbats while the others get the bouquets! Verse 11 explains that those who are punished, "it seems to us at the time something to make us sad, not glad. Later, however, those who have been disciplined by such punishment reap the peaceful reward of a righteous life."

And then just like that it all made sense to me. So while I may not exactly be at Big Dad's receiving end, it is also true that IF He loves me, cares for me and sees any kind of potential in me, He would try to push me harder till I qualify for the finals. Remember, some of the best athletes in the world are the ones who've been trained the hardest? They've been disciplined to take control of their health, diet, exercise, thoughts and even sex life! So why isn't everyone taken in to test their best? Well, let me be blunt here. "For many are called, but few are chosen," (*Matthew 22:14*). And the chosen few are those in whom the Lord sees potential. It's also true that not everyone will finish till the end (although I'd think Christ would love to see us win!), but it's our ability to push through those barriers, consistently, is what would impress Christ the most, and of course, with His help and guidance.

It's true that I (still) don't like being corrected and I can safely assume that I belong to the majority because most people don't… But in spite of some "wrong" personal choices I had made, had I not had these moments of isolation, which I can call my training period -- my life would have been very different today. Yes, I sorely miss the professional hiatus I once had, and the adulation and admirers that came as a bonus, but I wouldn't trade my current confidence and calm and proximity to Jesus for anything or anyone else.

Christ ground me down to make me someone who is truly humble, strong, independent, practical, yet sensitive.

If you knew me 10 years ago, you'd love me immediately but if you didn't truly love me, you'd slam your door on me just as immediately!

I am not saying, I have arrived in life. I still have numerous issues to work on, but I can safely say that in time I will get to those issues as well.

3

Confidence is underrated

Joshua 1:1-9

So before I begin sharing my personal thoughts on this Bible passage, which was once again received by me through *Our Daily Bread*, I'd like to touch upon the dialogue between God and Joshua in this particular chapter of the book of Joshua.

In these passages, we see that Joshua has been elevated into a leadership role after the death of Moses (and I hope that you're actually opening your Bibles and reading the verses mentioned above, as we go along). As soon as the mourning for Moses was finished, God spoke to Joshua and instructed him to lead the nation. Joshua recognized that to step forward and take up the reins except under God's immediate direction would have been presumptuous.

Although he had long been the designated successor, it still remained God's prerogative to guide the transition and formally confer authority upon Joshua. The speech we read in these verses is Joshua's coronation, as it were—his formal installation as the new head of the nation.

Three times in His commissioning of Joshua, God admonished him to have courage. The first time He was referring to the courage necessary to complete the task of conquering the land and dividing it among the tribes. The second time He was referring to the courage required to keep the law of Moses, disregarding all the pressures to compromise. He would have to maintain the law even when he saw advantages in sidestepping it—advantages in terms of his own convenience or popularity. The third time God spoke of courage, He was referring to it as the remedy for fear, and He emphasized His command to be fearless by twice rewording and repeating it.

It therefore becomes easy to understand that God's main purpose in speaking to Joshua was to allay all the fears natural to the heart of this new leader.

Now let's come back to the present times.

Haven't we all been in a situation like Joshua at least once or several times in our lives -- entrusted with a new responsibility, pressure to fulfill the expectations of those around us and literally feeling like a pack of boiled noodles, ready to collapse, yet looking all pret-a-manger on the outside?

     CONFIDENCE IS UNDERRATED

And this responsibility could be anything. Becoming a new mom, new wife, new employee, new immigrant, new student, new neighbor, new daughter-in-law… and the list goes on.

I felt pretty much the same as a new wife-mother-immigrant and all at once trying to adapt to a new identity. Easy? No. Well, for some this could have been a cake walk, but like I said earlier, we all have such different and unique identities and why certain issues or situations trigger a reaction in some, while has the exact opposite reaction in another – is a mystery that's going to need one more book!

Like Joshua, I wasn't ready to take on my new roles either. Yes, I was ecstatic to be a mother and I wouldn't have traded that for anything else in the world, but another part of me was so cut off from people outside or society that at times, even a simple act of going to do groceries seemed unthinkable. I had lost all my confidence. I would start getting awkward around people (due to post pregnancy weight gain), inability to follow Canadian accent and an acute sense of inferiority that comes from struggling to adapt to a new country and culture. And then I received Joshua 1 to latch on to.

For the first time in life, I truly experienced what a crushed sense of confidence could do to one's personality. It doesn't matter if you were once fiery like me and all that. It only takes one or some kind of a jab that life throws at you and sends you shaking from head to toe. My initial years in Canada was that jab. I was left to swim with no life guards, no life jackets and not even a remote piece of rubber ducky to hold on to. But there was someone watching me closely. He was there all along as I was learning to flap, gasp, stay afloat and largely just ensuring that I don't sink! And I didn't. And this book is a proof of that victory.

On a quiet summer evening, as verse 9, popped out in front of me, I knew there was someone swimming WITH me and gently holding my hands and feet because He wanted me to complete that stretch. This is all I needed to know, as He told me, "Remember that I have commanded you to be determined and confident! Don't be afraid or discouraged, for I, the Lord your God, am with you wherever you go," (*Verse 9*).

   CONFIDENCE IS UNDERRATED

4

This tough cookie called faith!

Romans 4:16-22

My favorite character in the Bible is Abraham. There are several other characters, who've impressed me from time to time, but this man's chromosomes are made of different stuff – if you know what I mean!

First, God decides to crack a little joke with this poor guy, asks him to sacrifice the son of his old age as an offering and then stops him from doing so, when this broken father is about to slay his son. Then this superhero is asked to uproot himself and his family from their familiar surroundings and move to a new land. It was a test of faith and obedience for a 75-year-old man. This Old Testament Hall of Fame candidate, doesn't flinch even a bit and does exactly what he was told. He went out, even though he did not know where he was going (God did have a sense of humor with this guy, right?)

Now, if these seven verses touched my heart personally, there must be a reason and some point that God was trying to drive home to me. But I wasn't going to give in easily. First of all I lacked complete submission on giving up on my one and only most beloved possession and secondly, I had no patience for God's promises to be fulfilled after many and many years of waiting. So what next? Well, like we all know… sometimes, there's no other way but to trust God. And in case, you decide not to, there's still no other way, but to trust God! Because, at times, that's THE only way God wants us to operate. So trusting Him doesn't become an option, it becomes a necessity. Verse 16 says, "And so the promise was based on faith, in order that the promise should be guaranteed as God's free gift to all of Abraham's descendants – not just to those who obey the Law, but also to those who believe as Abraham did…" The bad news is that obedience alone is not enough, but the good news is that if and when faith and obedience come together, they become a deadly combo to reap rewards from God. There is a reason why Abraham is called "father of many nations," (*Verse 17*).

There were times (still are) when I sought desperate answers to many a questions. The whys and the hows rage so heavily inside me that at times, it's difficult to focus on God's plans for me. That's when verse 21 comes handy, "He

 THIS TOUGH COOKIE CALLED FAITH!

was absolutely sure that God would be able to do what he had promised." So, God really does want us to go back and think. Am. I. Absolutely. Sure?

I want what I want and I want it... now! It is difficult to trust in a plan that required us to surrender all control of the time for completion.

In order to trust in God, you and I are required to totally surrender our will, our ideas, our desires, and our future in to God's hands. I was a control freak and didn't want to give the control of any part of my life over to another. If you don't believe that God loves you fully and really does have your best interests at heart and desires the very best for you, trusting Him is going to be extremely difficult. It takes a very special relationship to allow that measure of surrender. Most of us have a tendency to claim trust in God. However, at the first sign of any difficulty or trial, we think that God does not love us because He is allowing this difficulty to happen. The trial is exactly what God is using to test the level of trust that we have in Him.

Quite ironical right? Well, it took me a lot of time to fathom that. Faith really is the hardest reality of Christian life, but if we can even do half of what is expected out of us, we'd be well on our way to greater victories.

I mean it.

5

When in trouble call 9115

Psalms 91:9-16

911 – the emergency help line that runs across North America is helpful, or so I believe. Okay, it actually is and I have no intention to doubt their immediate ability to rescue those who need help. But, it's not for everything and everyone who needs a rescue!

One day when I and a cab driver got into a scuffle – he threatened to push me out of the taxi, with my son – who was two-years-old then. Fearful and panicking, I called 911 to complain about the situation. So this is a gist of how our conversation went:

Me: (*narrate the entire cab incident*)

Operator: Ma'am, is this a life and death emergency?

Me: Well, not exactly, but the driver has pulled the
            car in the middle of nowhere and threatens to
            drive my toddler and me out.

Operator: Ma'am, is this a life and death emergency?

Me: Ah… Not exactly. Thankfully! But, we need
            help. This is harassment…

Operator: Ma'am, is this a life and death emergency?

Me: Okay. No. But…

Operator: So, you need to hang up coz there might be
            someone else trying to call, who might be dying.

(*Click*)

Humiliated? Yes. Embarrassed? Yes. Disappointed? Yes.

THANKFULLY, Jesus doesn't turn us down. He does not filter our calls on the basis of life and death. He does not ignore our plea for help – no matter how little or insignificant it may be. When I read and re read Psalms 91: 9-16, I was filled with a deep sense of reassurance that no matter how I was or what my issues were in life, He was there with me. God says, "I will save those who love me and will protect those who acknowledge me as Lord," (*Verse 14*). "When they call to me, I will answer them; when they are in trouble, I will be with them. I will rescue them and honor them," (*Verse 15*).

There is a reason why Psalms 91 is actually one of the most popular Bible chapters and will continue to be. It carries with it the perfect promise of protection, safety and well-being that is so encouraging that by the time you reach the end of this Psalm, you feel like a certain load is lifted off you. At least that's how I felt when I read these verses or timely remembered them in the midst of a crisis that could have turned ugly or even as a 14-year-old. Yes there's a story behind that too.

My mother read out Psalms 91 to me the day I gave my Math exam and came back home crying! Math and I were literally like David and Goliath. And not knocking this numerical Goliath down meant repeating an entire year of that grade. I did manage to bring this giant down, while trusting as a teenager that whatever my mother read to me that afternoon was the ultimate truth.

I still remember the rush I felt through my entire body as I innocently tugged on to the belief that "I will pass Math exam," and I surely did.

So you know what, don't complicate your faith in the Lord or intellectualize it (like I do)… Just have a simple, no nonsense, blind-brainless faith. Yes. I am going to repeat that – blind-brainless faith! Because when you read Psalms 91, you will know that He's our ultimate protector and that He really does keep our life together.

6

Make your choices

2 Peter 1:2-11

The reason why these verses grabbed my attention is because of the multiple choices offered here. Sometimes I feel, life would be easier and definitely less complicated if we had no choices or the concept of freewill did not exist. When I am stuck between a black and a pink or a vegetable skillet and noodle soup, I often point two fingers at my son, ask him to pick one and whichever he does, is my ordre du jour! Unfortunately, in life, this innocent game doesn't come handy.

If we start reading Verses 5 onwards, there is a whole list of things, we are required to add to our existing qualities. "For this very reason, make every effort to add to your faith goodness; and to goodness, knowledge; and to knowledge, self-control; and to self-control, perseverance; and to perseverance, godliness; and to godliness, mutual affection; and to mutual affection, love (*Verses 5-7*).

So let's list these attributes down one by one.

1. Faith
2. Goodness
3. Knowledge
4. Self-control
5. Perseverance
6. Godliness
7. Mutual affection
8. Love

Not only does God want us to have this 1-8 order, He also wants us to keep adding on to each of the existing qualities. So let's say, I can't just have Faith. I need to enhance my faith with 2-8 order. Or I can't just be happy with having a terrific Self-control, this quality needs to be added and enhanced with Faith, Goodness, Knowledge, Self-control, Perseverance, Godliness, Mutual affection and Love.

These verses force me to think that life can never quite be one-directional or we simply cannot live with a shade of black and white. That's not how God designed this world to be. He wants us to experience, see and feel multiple shades of black and 1,000 other white-color varieties and even mix them together and see what comes out of it. Confused? Well, it's easy to understand it this way. Every single day of our life

                                    MAKE YOUR CHOICES

we can't just wear one set of clothes… when there's winter, we're expected to slip into a jacket and when there's heat, we're expected to strip down our clothing. Imagine wearing the same clothes irrespective of any weather?

Now similarly imagine having only Godliness as our quality – we read Bible five times a day, pray for two hours every four times a day, offer our tithes, go to church every Sunday and even spend time praising and worshiping God – diligently! But if we lack the faith in Christ and possess no knowledge of what we're doing or why we're doing and get angry at the drop of a hat, yell at our kids and get into an argument with those who love us or start cursing God when things go wrong, instead of sticking to perseverance… clinging on to His feet and most importantly, if we simply cannot love ourselves or others – how will we ever be active and effective (*Verse 8*)?

It's an eye-opener for me to realize that because we do not follow the 1-8 order or pick and choose the quality or qualities that suit us the most, we keep forgetting that we have already been purified of our past sins (*Verse 9*). God has already forgiven us and it is WE who cling on to things of the past. Disturbing experiences from the past. Bad memories from the past. Even bad behavior from the past.

God has wiped our slate clean, however, since He has given us the gift of freewill, He wants *us* to rewire our brain to believe that if we try just a bit harder, to make God's call and His choice of you a permanent experience. If you did that, you'd never abandon your faith (*Verse 10*)!

7

Go to Him

Psalms 3

When bad time strikes, we could be more than tempted to seek "outside" help, especially when things between you and God are going rather "slow and unpleasant." So what does that mean? That just means one thing – when we're not finding quick answers to our prayers, there is a possibility that we begin to doubt our faith.

I have found myself in the midst of this turmoil way too many times too. And I wouldn't deny – I have been tempted. Tempted to give up on God. Give Him a break. Try self-help books. Even go to the extent of figuring out if God is really alive. Yes, that makes me sound like a horrible person. Someone who is totally lost and has shaky or no faith or someone who doesn't trust with the trust of a child. All this might be true for me, actually. And I have no qualms in confessing that I haven't exactly been a good believer. I have ever too often blown hot and blown cold. Fortunately and thankfully, my insecurities and fear of ending up all alone in this big empty world has always made me stick around with (negative) people longer than I should and that very negative trait has made me stick around with God too. So if I could do that with negative people, why not with God? I have been all too scared with the idea of leaving Him and trying out something or someone else, other than Him. You might think of this as a "commitment" with God. Actually, it's not. I wish I had other options, but I don't. In my mind, I am convinced that Jesus is the only option for me. And therefore my best option too. Whatever way it works… as long as it works!

So that brings me back to Psalms 3. These eight powerful verses came flying past me when I was beginning to believe that I am done for good. The social isolation was killing me and so was my inability to use my skills professionally. And precisely at that very minute, He reassured me by telling me that He answers my cry for help from His sacred hill (*Verse 4*). I feel so better even *now* when I scramble to finish off this chapter and go back to reading this verse several times. It's like a sudden mind shift that comes from being aware that someone *is* looking over you. You're anything but alone.

Furthermore, verses 5 and 6, totally unstitch me, "I lay down and slept; I awoke, for the Lord sustained me.

I will not be afraid of ten thousands of people who have set themselves against me all around." What's important to note here is that *you can* literally lie down and sleep because God is with you. It's a blessing to be able to sleep even in the midst of life's turmoil. If you don't know what I mean, ask those who depend heavily on sleeping pills just to get those eight hours tucked in.

And even when you have enemies (I am not talking about people you keep getting into arguments with. I am referring to those who try to cause you serious harm, with no fault of yours) as living people or your own negative traits that hinder your growth, you know that you can safely stand up to all this – simply because Lord is with you.

And most importantly, it was humbling for me to remember that victory comes from the Lord (*Verse 8*). No matter how hard I tried, every effort to straighten out my life would be wasted if I didn't shout out to the Lord to make me a winner. Whether you like it or not, only HE has that power.

In conclusion, Psalms 3 renders me speechless and also strangely comforted. It is enough for me to know that if David could think of God as his helper, protector and punisher – then who am I to question these promises!

8

The Master of all Promises

Isaiah 66:12-14

And since there are only three verses in this chapter that stood up for attention – I needn't say more – other than this that these are the three most powerful verses in the history of mankind. You can chew them. Cling on to them. Hold them fast. Keep them close. Read them 10 times a day. Paste them on your wall. Hide them under your pillow… Do whatever that needs to be done, but oh boy! I can tell you that there was no greater promise than the promise Lord has offered in Isaiah 66: 12-14.

Ever experienced the pain of being so tired and helpless in life that you have no willingness to go any further? Well, the Israelites too knew this bone-tiredness. However, in Isaiah 66 God offers a solution with a promise. The Israelites had suffered through the exile, cut off from their land and from their God. Then, when some were allowed to return in anticipation of the great blessings they had been promised, they found only further suffering. The small groups of exiles who returned to Judah after Persia's defeat of Babylon in 539 faced hardship, famine, political in-fighting, and economic oppression. Their weariness, after generations of oppression and humiliation, must have been unbearable.

And because I am a mother, I understand the importance of providing a nurturing, comforting care to my child. And since we're God's own children, He promises the same care for us. Joy and comfort. Milk and water. Weary bones refreshed and restored. In the midst of the thundering of condemnation and retribution, it is this quiet passage of maternal care and human delight that gestures more particularly to the presence of God with God's people that their bone-tired bodies and spirits might flourish again, like the grass.

At a more simplistic level – I read these verses when I am sick because here, God promises to provide strength and health (*Verse 14*). I read these verses when I feel I have no one to help me in this foreign land because here, He is volunteering to help (*Verse 14*) and when I just need to feel comforted, in general, I dig out these verses.

So hold tight. I have nothing more to say in this chapter except for the fact that when He promises, He really means it. If you want to test drive this. Do it. Feel the difference

     THE MASTER OF ALL PROMISES

just when you start saying out these verses to yourself loud and clear.

Lord's backing you by promising:

1. Prosperity
2. Wealth
3. Love
4. Comfort
5. Gladness
6. Strength
7. Health
8. Help

Go. Find these power words in the three verses and underline them for you to go back to whenever you're in a desperate need for some reassurance.

9

My new *kurta*

Revelations 21:1-7

By this time during the writing of my book, I had to take yet another brief hiatus before I could start punching my laptop keys again. If I mention the reason(s) many would start loading me the theory of "just be happy… Live life. Go out, do something. You're wasting your life. This is one life. Blah blah blah and blah…"

While I am NOT disrespecting any of these propositions and well-meaning suggestions and I genuinely do think that that's coming from a space of concern, love or frustration (because people who've known me for many years have known me as a fire brand or more precisely a go-getter!) but what do you do when your brain truly and quite automatically begins to crumble? So you want to do things but can't do those things. For many months, I struggled between the strongholds of WANT and CAN'T. Have you seen a person get affected by ALS? My best friend would say, "You're making it sound more intense than it really is, Rash!" But, hey, no. Let's come back to the point. Have you really seen a person with ALS? If you did or have heard of one, you'd know that their ability to do things diminishes bit by bit. One step after another closer to hell and disability. Their organs don't stop functioning in one bang of a moment... It goes one chitty chitty bang bang and then chitty chitty and then bang bang and then chit and bang and boom... The organ loses its function. But all this happens slowly. I have seen a close friend suffer and I know that he WANTS to stand up and walk but he CAN'T. It's a tussle between wanting to preserve those few precious cells that would never regenerate themselves versus your heart nudging you to take that little walk on the wet grass or go running towards your li'l pup who's waiting to be kissed. But in reality, you can do neither. Your body is weak. And your mental and physical strength is waning off.

So when I started seeking therapy to make sense of my life or to get my anxiety bouts and stress under control, my therapist pointed towards the losses in my life. And according to him, loss of identity is one of the top five losses, next to death, that could put any person under grief and trauma. To put it briefly, I didn't know who I was anymore. The absence of whatever I held dear professionally and personally and starting life all over again had caused such an upheaval in my life that I did feel like my ALS friend – wasting away one chit, one bang at a time. And that's exactly when God intervened and didn't let the boom happen. And that's why Revelations 21: 1-7 becomes all the more relevant in my life.

By far Revelations is one of the most powerful and enigmatic chapters in the entire Bible. And I say that because it possesses in itself the power to run a human life in its present and future form. But at this point in time, I'm only going to pick what's relevant to my life. And *Verse 5* here is like a hand in glove. "He who was seated on the throne said, "I am making everything new!" Then he said, "Write this down, for these words are trustworthy and true.""

Verse 5 and the concluding verses till *Verse 7* carry a strong message of encouragement. Christ's kingdom has been established and the process of restoration has begun. The rest of *Verse 5* continues with further assurance. "Write this down, for these words are trustworthy and true." God's word is true and can be trusted. Christ is reigning on the throne. We are looking forward to this promise, guaranteed by God, that we will receive the eternal blessings and rewards for being faithful to Him through grief, crying, pain, suffering, and death.

While we continue to look at the word NEW in most of these verses with a magnifying glass, I want to divert a bit and draw your attention to the title of this chapter (if that hasn't intrigued you already). A friend has been trying to grill into my brain the significance of wearing a "new *kurta*" (Indian style shirt). "Throw away your old tattered *kurta* and endorse the new *kurta* that Christ has made for you Rashmi *ji*," he would often repeat. Poetic right? All that suffix of *ji* and *kurta* and all… But to me it's profound. Especially as I sit and meditate upon Revelation 21 over and over again, all this *kurta* metaphor – both old and new – makes sudden sense!

If we are a new creation in Christ (*Verse 5*) it is indeed time to throw away the old rugged *kurta* and exchange it for a new crisp white shirt with blue denims… Or whatever is YOUR favorite attire (I just mentioned mine!)

And then I remember the words of my therapist as he mulls over ways to restore my "lost identity." However, the flood lights in my mind just went off as God revealed to me a simple logic – if my identity is lost, so is my *kurta* – but here God is literally assuring me that He'll make all things new and logically, my identity is also new. Right? And if my identity IS new, I am no longer eligible or fit to wear what I used to, but instead He's providing me my favorite white shirt and denim.

Are you ready to let go of your *kurta*?

10

Suffering is good!

1 Peter 3:8-17

To be honest, these 10 verses are loaded with life lessons. They're so simple and self-explanatory that sharing my personal thoughts on these verses would be kinda unfair. Yet I am going to make an attempt because sometimes, the simplest of things are the toughest to grasp and hardest to do.

Starting from *Verse 8* that stresses on loving one another and being kind and humble and so on and so forth and as we reflect further the verses continue with switching curses with blessings, speaking no evil or lies and striving for peace. My point is – how many of us really endorse this? And in all honesty, most of us – don't. And that's why Christians can oftentimes end up being some of the meanest people in the world. No, I'm not saying cruelest because we don't go around shedding blood or causing violence… however as Christians, we're quick enough to judge, condone someone and convict that person even before God can peep into that person's life. Aren't we all guilty of doing this to our friends, family or even fellow Christians whom we bump into church Sunday-to Sunday!

And yet in *Verse 12* it is clearly written that the Lord watches over the righteous and listens to their prayers but opposes those who do evil. However, we're so conditioned to do exactly that – evil!

Here, for some reason, my focus keeps drifting back to the way we treat each other in church. In my personal experience (and I don't mean to be judgmental) people rock and clap on worship songs, close their eyes and lift their hands in Hallelujah and genuinely seem to form that spiritual connection with God. I have nothing against that, but the moment this camaraderie comes to an end and you're out of your "worship zone" we immediately switch gears into a territory that God clearly says He "opposes." We gossip, judge, make remarks about someone that may or may not be true… and even if it's true, why gossip about it? Does all this sound familiar to you? Have you personally been guilty of wreaking havoc in someone's life just because of gossip? Well, you don't have to tell me but tell yourself – have you really been living that life that God wants from you? I haven't. And I am guilty of that. On the contrary, I used to think, gossip was a really cool thing – because I was never the victim!

Verse 15 onwards, Christ is asking us to do what we SHOULD DO and not what we should NOT do. There's a difference, read on: *(Verse 15),* But in your hearts revere Christ as Lord. Always be prepared to give an answer to everyone who asks you to give the reason for the hope that you have. But do this with gentleness and respect, *(Verse 16)* keeping a clear conscience, so that those who speak maliciously against your good behavior in Christ may be ashamed of their slander. *(Verse 17)* For it is better, if it is God's will, to suffer for doing good than for doing evil.

But these last three powerful verses of *1 Peter: 3* can only be accomplished if and only if we try to do what Christ actually wants us to do. And that is: simply loving one another, being kind and humble with one another and paying back cursing with blessing.

I am not saying it's easy to do. It's next to impossible to love someone who's hurt us and caused us deep pain. It's really tough to be kind to someone if we're oblivious to our own follies or weaknesses. In this situation, we'd think of ourselves as victim and which again is a natural human psyche.

But, our reward is right there.

I am going to flip some verses for the sake of our understanding (and it's purely my interpretation). Let's read *Verse 12* that clearly mentions: For the eyes of the Lord are

   SUFFERING IS GOOD!

on the righteous and **his ears are attentive to their prayer,** but the face of the Lord is against those who do evil.

What I have written in bold is million dollar.

Simple because what could be a greater reward for you and me than having Christ take personal interest in our prayers!

11

Are we ready yet?

Galatians 6:1-10

As I sit at my desk, writing, my mind races back to "church politics," yes CHURCH POLITICS. So, in this chapter, I am not going to add nothing new really but pick up from the previous chapter.

For the first time when I got these special verses from *Galatians 6: 1-10*, I had a different interpretation of these scriptures… now when I re read them, the Holy Spirit is guiding me to share with you something that I'd not initially planned.

To me, these verses are all about how we should treat others. In fact, they're screaming out loud about our conduct towards others.

And please don't get me wrong... I am not anti-church or church goers, I am just puzzled by a simple observation that some of the people who call themselves most pious are the first ones to point a finger at others. Church or Christ snobbery is another thing I have noticed is most rampant in our Christian society. Take for example a time when I tried befriending a church pastor here in Edmonton. An immigrant like me, 60 plus, wears Christ's love on his sleeve and if you do not visit his church – he takes a personal offence to that. So one day when I decided to get some spiritual guidance from him, his first statement to me was – "are you a born again Christian?" Ok, what if I am not? Are you not going to help me? And what if I am? Are you going to help me any better? Whether I sought help from this preacher, is hardly a guess!

Once again, with due respect to our churches, pastors and institutions and individuals who run the "show" I am no one to judge or blame anyone... But it is purely my interpretation that people new in faith are often segregated as those who "know too little" or often snubbed for having "little faith" or as those whose lives need to change only if they're "reborn." My argument is – help them then. Because the very first verse (*Verse 1*) says, "Brothers and sisters, if someone is caught in a sin, you who live by the Spirit should restore that person gently. But watch yourselves, or you also may be tempted." That clearly doubles up the responsibility for those in positions of authority.

Interestingly, society might think we're oblivious to how

we treat people but my personal belief is that we all know exactly HOW we treat people… We just choose to let our egos cover our shortcomings. And my understanding might not be too far from what the Bible says in (*Verse 7*) "Do not deceive yourselves; no one makes a fool of God. You will reap exactly what you sow."

Like I had said during the beginning of this chapter, there is nothing much I want to contribute here. But if you've come this far in the book then you're on board with me and I'd urge you just one thing, as (*Verse 10*) says, "Therefore, as we have opportunity, let us do good to all people, especially to those who belong to the family of believers."

As believers, our responsibility doubles up to draw a person new in faith – closer to God – not push them away from God.

12

Why are you jealous anyway?

Psalms 37:1-8

Sometimes I wonder – why is it that people who do evil – flourish. And oftentimes we notice that this really is the way of the world. In a more standard or linear way of looking at things, we do notice that those who plot, scheme, connive and plan are the happier ones. While those who are genuinely innocent, flawless and naïve are the ones who suffer the most. This might sound like self-praise – but not necessarily – because people with the latter traits could also be considered stupid and I certainly belong to that category.

But this powerful psalm is laden with a promise that is so real that even if you don't want to believe it (and it's only human, not to), the least you can do is put your trust out in Christ and see the miracle roll automatically. And I can vouch for it because I am the living proof of that.

So if you're like me and belong to the latter category, you've hope!

For the longest period in my life I had a hard time forgiving those who'd caused me pain. I held on to the bitter memories. Sad times. Mentally replayed all those moments which I couldn't let go of. Worst is I saw those very people who'd hurt me prosper in status, finance, power or even love and they seem to have everything going right for them. And on the other hand – it was me – wallowing in misery and having a little pity party.

I found myself asking God why He chose to be super kind to those who believe in hurting and harming people... as a matter of fact, I was quite upset spiritually and found myself losing interest each time I sat down to pray or read the Bible.

And then it was one of those days where I was struggling really hard to let go. I wanted an answer and I was not going to get away without having one. And like I'd said earlier, I'm a living example of someone that proves that God TALKS to us.

So just like that, *Psalms 37:1-8* popped open in front of me. Here, *Verse 7* says, "Be still before the Lord and wait patiently for him, do not fret when people succeed in their ways, when they carry out their wicked schemes."

   WHY ARE YOU JEALOUS ANYWAY?

Was I going to trust this verse? Well, did I have a choice?

I was such a disbeliever that once I'd told a spiritual leader in India that Christianity has no meaning in my life. "Jesus is inactive. He's so passive."

Don't hold these statements against me. I know they can offend the sentiments of any true believer but you'd be happy to know that it was JESUS Himself who helped me to change my views about Him. Yes, He cared enough to do that. Handle me separately. Handle me "passively" and gave me enough importance especially when in the bigger scheme of things – I am just a tiny little human – on planet Earth and tinier in the entire galaxy that He's so aptly created! But Jesus took notice of ME. Yes ME. I'm so obscure, yet He chose to give me enough importance to let me know that through *Verse 7*.

And at this moment, that's all I want you to know as well. If He could do it for me, He could do it for you too. Because, if He did it for someone else, He could do it for me and I literally hung on to this belief with my dear life.

During this time, my other big revelation was that by focusing on what others have and I don't... I was pushing away whatever little that I had. So technically speaking I was turning my blessing into a curse. How God chooses to bless those who cause others pain – is totally between God and them. I cannot turn around to tell God that He should punish the mean guys out there because... they're mean! Well, God created those mean guys too. They too are His children and how He deals with them is really His choice. That's really not my jurisdiction.

If we think we're believers, our main job is to forgive and move on.

And I'll digress a bit here because a lot of people say "we can forgive but not forget!" I don't buy that theory. Because in principle, forgiving IS forgetting. How? Does Christ say that when He chooses to forgive our sins, He'll just forgive them but always be mindful of how we went wrong or the horrible things we've done on a sly? Both you and I know that each one of us has hidden dark secrets that only you and you know of! And of course besides you, God knows those little dirty secrets too (wakey wakey!) But He still chooses to forgive us for that. Right?

And if He doesn't remember the horrible things we've done behind closed doors, then who are we to remember the horrible things others have done to us and never apologized for it? I'm not saying it's easy. Certainly not. It's tough. But that's exactly what my concluding verse says, "Refrain from anger and turn from wrath; do not fret—it leads only to evil *(Verse 8)*."

Not letting go of things leads to anger and anger leads to wrath and wrath leads to evil. Isn't it so logical? So sequential?

Think about what I'm saying the next time you decide to hold on to that bitterness towards someone for too long. Or jump in fury because your "mean" girlfriend found the right man, while you're still busy looking for a bride's maid outfit!

      WHY ARE YOU JEALOUS ANYWAY?

13

They'll fail you, like they always do

Jeremiah 17:5-10

For the longest time I relied on my friends and parents for almost anything and everything in life. And that's lovely isn't it? But God wanted it another way for me. If I had my way, I'd be so self-absorbed in my own "good luck" of friends running to help me when a tire is flat, when I lose road direction, miswrite a bank cheque, need emotional support or simply want someone to have tea with. And that was my life and I was so happy with that. I was clearly wearing my mojo on my sleeves. And that sense of shelter and my cocooned vision of the world was leading to my arrogance. It's funny how people I've known for many years have started confessing to me, "You were one helluva woman, girl. All arrogant, snobbish, proud..." Yeah bring it on baby! I was a lot of that and more. But could I escape from God? Well... We all know the deal!

The reason I chose *Jeremiah 17:5-10* is because its verses would make perfect sense to those who are like me – deeply dependent on everyone around them – but their own selves - for every little thing. While people love you and do not want to disappoint you, the other reason why being dependent on people for anything is such a bad idea because people are people after all. They have their own lives, they can get tired, angry, sad, bored or simply don't feel like being there for someone all the time (it doesn't mean they're bad, it just means they're as human as you are).

So when your own expectations of them are not met, it leads to disappointment. It doesn't mean you should set lower standards of expectations. That's not healthy! I've often heard people say, "Expect very little from others. The more you expect. The more you're bound to get hurt." I don't buy that theory at all. If you are a human, you are born to expect. Even not expecting, is an expectation. Doesn't Jesus expect from us?

The point is not to NOT expect, the point is how not to over or under expect and how to communicate your expectations in the most healthy and respectful way. You need to set your own boundaries and pray to know if you're right in expecting something. Should you even expect what you're expecting, and if you're convinced about being on

     THEY'LL FAIL YOU, LIKE THEY ALWAYS DO

the right track, seek God's help to make the right move. And like I have been saying right throughout – trust me it works – and I'm a living proof of that.

I did digress from my main topic and the point here is not about giving you a dummies guide to, "expect right and feel right," but the rambling does bring me to my main point and that is: PUT YOUR TRUST IN GOD. Let me say this one more time, put your trust IN GOD.

Let's go back to *Jeremiah 17:5-10* and let's take the first verse, "Cursed is the one who trusts in man, who draws strength from mere flesh and whose heart turns away from the Lord." This verse could be interpreted in a million different ways, but for me the interpretation of putting your trust in man instead of God, makes complete sense (and it's also quite literal!) And why is it so hurtful when every single time we trust someone else other than God? Well, here's the answer in *Verse 9*, "The heart is deceitful above all things and beyond cure. Who can understand it?"

So I am by no means challenging the love and care my friends or your family has for you. All that is genuine and as real as my first streak of grey hair. But remember, man can fail, God can never! And I'm going to tone down *Verse 9* for our understanding. A simple google search for synonyms of the word "deceitful" led me to these result (try it on your own while you're reading the book): dishonest, untruthful, mendacious, insincere, false, disingenuous, untrustworthy, unscrupulous, unprincipled, two-faced, Janus-faced, duplicitous, double-dealing, underhanded, crafty, cunning, sly, scheming, calculating, treacherous, Machiavellian, sneaky, tricky, foxy, crooked and more…

Again, this by no way implies that we or our loved ones are any of these but our human heart can experience all or any of these emotions at any given time – all at once – or one emotion at a time! And I will prove my point with the help of this very simple example. You wait for a friend to call you. But she does not return the call you so eagerly awaited. You wanted to outpour your emotions, tell her all about how bitchy your boss was, how insecure your boyfriend has become, how manipulative your neighbor's been blah blah blah… But the fact is your friend has other priorities to fulfill and she doesn't call. So you call her and tell her as gently as you can that you waited on her the previous night. Your friend is all guilty and sorry and tries to tell you how busy she really was. How slammed she was with the demands of her new boss/love interest/weight loss blah blah and blah…

Now the point here is:

- Was the friend really that busy? Did she not take pee breaks??

- Did she not think her friend had a need to share and so she should have been more available?

- It could also be that the friend is bored of listening to the same problems over and over again???

    THEY'LL FAIL YOU, LIKE THEY ALWAYS DO

Now you do match-the-following. Start putting the most appropriate synonyms that are mentioned above to these three questions I've posed.

And you'll be surprised to know that almost all or most of these words will find the right fit with the right sentence.

So basically if there's one single thing you can take away from this entire chapter, it should be that before you run to anyone for anything – in your happiest or saddest moment – pause. Yes pause, because the other person may or may not be as excited or as sad. May not even have the time or inclination for a follow-up on how well you're dealing with your emotions (unless they're paid for it).

But you know what? Every single time you turn to Jesus and since I am a repeater, let me repeat this – EVERY SINGLE TIME you turn TO JESUS, He's there to hear you out. Like my eyes are peeled on Ayaan every single time he's playing in the midst of 50 of other kids… I know exactly how my son squeals, shouts, laughs and calls out for me… I tell ya, Jesus knows that about you and me way more than I know about my son. Because we just reproduced our babies (sorry for being so literal!) but Jesus created us. Bone by bone. Blood vein by blood vein. Cell by cell. Hair by hair. Organ by organ!

Will Jesus not listen to you when you shout out for Him?

14

He's got your back!

Lamentations 3:19-33

Out of everything that I have shared with you so far, these verses from *Lamentations 3* have the deepest and profoundest impact on me. It makes me sit up, gives me goosebumps, makes me leave everything at hand and simply divert every ounce of my energy to read and re read these verses… that's the kind of impact I am talking about. Why? Well, I am going to tell you all about it in just a few minutes.

If you know anything about my life, you'd also know that my life has not exactly been one of the easiest. Like someone who's lost a limb would say, "Are you just crying because you lost a relationship?" Or someone who has serious mental illness would chuckle, "Know what it means to live on pills to fix your bipolar?" True. I wouldn't know any of this.

But let me tell you, we all have our own demons to fight. Behind closed doors, monsters can do a double flip, grow extra horns and a longer tail and make mental tattoos of - isolation, loneliness, poverty, divorce, unwanted pregnancy, betrayal, joblessness, sexual abuse or loss of identity – with a sharper needle and darker ink! And trust you me, these tattoos can be just as telling as losing a limb or bipolar.

We really do have our own demons to fight, some are just more conspicuous than the others.

After moving to Canada, my loss of identity was so acute that I couldn't associate with myself or my body anymore. I was used to being looked at as "a hot and happening" "journalist," "radio jockey," "writer…" Here, no one really cared what I wrote or said or thought. For the largest part of my life in Canada I couldn't detach myself with who I was. Was I even me? Was I even there? That thought pained me. It made me anxious. Depressed. Dejected. After spending 10 years being a journalist in India, no one needed me now. I was useless. A waste. Or so I thought.

It took me just equal amount of time to know that God didn't think of me that way. So did I turn to God on my own? Yes and no. I was a born Christian but never took pride in calling myself one. I don't have an Anglican name. I don't "look" Christian. My friends are non-Christians. I worked in the secular world. And I hated this concoction of an identity. Why was Christianity forced on me when nothing about or around me was C-H-R-I-S-T-I-A-N!!???

Yes, I went to the church and read Bible every now and then and that was that.

Now I sit back and laugh at the way I thought. Yes I was also younger and stupider and that made matters worse.

I'd love to believe that Jesus was clearly offended and cared enough to prove to me that my identity was not defined by my non-Anglican name and looks or my profession or my loving non-Christian friends or my perfectly toned body that I always prided me (I was 20 kilos up after my son's birth!)

So it was a relationship of convenience but then I EVENTUALLY FELL IN LOVE (I had not meant to uppercase this. I wrote these lines and then realized. God's plan, I guess!) So I'd nowhere else to go, I decided to turn to Christ. But my sixth sense tells me, He did this on purpose. Jesus really wanted me to look out for Him. So He created circumstances for me under which He did come to my rescue like a dry leaf for an ant.

Verses 19 and 20 resonate so well with me… my spirit really was depressed. All the freakin' time. But you know what? All that freakin' time, Jesus got my back. I didn't realise it then, but I can tell you with absolute proof and belief that He did look out for me.

And technically that's what the Bible says too. *Verse 21* reminds us of a hope that keeps returning, "when I remember:" (*Verses 22-26*)

22 Because of the Lord's great love we are not consumed, for his compassions never fail.

23 They are new every morning; great is your faithfulness.

24 I say to myself, "The Lord is my portion; therefore I will wait for him.

25 The Lord is good to those whose hope is in him, to the one who seeks him;

26 It is good to wait quietly for the salvation of the Lord.

Yes sometimes life is not easy, like it never is for many of us but trust in our Lord is really the only way forward. And as clichéd as it may sound and as frustrating as it may be… when everything else fails, trust in Jesus and move forward. To sum it up, I am going to quote an excerpt of a conversation I once had with a God's man and how that stayed with me, many years after. And how relevant this can be for you and me.

Rashmi (Me): I might try an alternative religion…

God's Man (GM): And then?

Me: Then… nothing. Just follow what their practices are…

GM: And is there a guarantee everything in life will be rainbows and unicorn afterwards?

Me: Well… I dunno unless I try!

GM: So it really is about giving something a chance?

Me (sobbing): Yeah may be.

GM: Then how about you try Christ first? Try Him because what else can you do really other than trying Him out?

Me: (rolls eyes)

Now isn't that true for most of us? What else can we do but give God a chance? It's like an infant who is either fed by the mother or gone hungry...

So I decided not to go hungry and I was too scared to be fed by the social services, so I made a decision to eat or drink (more aptly). Be fed by the mother. Not by charity or foster parents!

Do you get my point?

15

Carry on with your life, while He works

Joshua 5:13-6:5

This Bible passage is perhaps the hardest to interpret and also the easiest to understand. But that is only if and once you understand. So I really had to go through this chapter many a times to get a better grasp of what was being said. Like you've noticed by now - conventional interpretation of these verses is not what I am going for.

For starters, let's focus on the first five verses of *Joshua 5*. I wish I could have touched a bit on the background but that would take me away from the primary focus of this chapter. So let's just assume that Joshua has an important task at hand. Let's picture him as a man on a mission with his mind all wrapped up with concerns about something he needs to accomplish professionally and personally. We all have been in this situation right? So it's not really that hard to understand Joshua's role here. And in the midst of all this, he looks up to see a man standing with a sword. What kind of picture does this bring to mind and what does it mean? Standing with any weapon drawn is a military position of one who either stands guard or who stands ready to go against an enemy.

Joshua doesn't stop at that and goes on to enquire if "that man" is "one of our soldiers, or an enemy?" (*Verse 13*)

Here Joshua quite interestingly projects the typical mindset of a man under threat or facing anxiety. We tend to see the battles we face as our battles and the forces we face as forces PERSONALLY against us.

And while I am no theologian or priest, I am going to dare to dissect this further.

"This man" replies in *Verse 14*: "Neither." He answers, "I indeed come now as captain of the host of the Lord." The answer comes in two parts. The first answer is simply a flat "neither." Interestingly, this man could have said that he's there for Joshua or Israel, but in essence, what his answer suggests is that he was not there to take sides. Neither Joshua's nor the enemy's.

The second part of the answer (*Verse 14*) gives the reason. In other words, "I am here, not to take sides, but to take over and take charge as commander of the Lord's army."

The first point proven here is that it was not for Joshua to claim which side God was on. No matter how right and holy it might be. Rather, the need was for Joshua to acknowledge God's presence.

And isn't this true of how we tend to approach our battles in life? We often work backwards. We turn things all around and plead God to support us rather than to submit and follow Him. Often, we forget that these battles are a joint venture. And just as Joshua was expected to submit, take orders, and rest the battle in God's hands – we are expected if not anointed – to do the same.

The second point here is that the Lord was also reminding Joshua of His personal presence, along with His powerful provision.

As we go further down *Verse 14*, we read how Joshua responded. "Joshua fell on his face to the earth, and bowed down, and said to him, "What has my lord to say to his servant?""

Joshua's humble surrender is a great metaphor for our own response to Lord's direct involvement and instructions to us. Do we get into the mode of submission as quickly as Joshua did?

The poignant question here is: DO WE REALLY LET GOD FIGHT THE BATTLE FOR US?

Through Joshua's humble act of submission we can rest assured that we never have to bear our burdens alone or face our enemies alone. Joshua was to know that the battles ahead and the entire conquest of Canaan was really God's conflict. What is our part?

What further blows my mind away is that Joshua along with his soldiers are instructed to (*Chapter 6:3*) "march around the city once a day for six days." Doesn't that signify fun? To me it does. God really wants us to have fun on purpose or feel the fun as we have it or he literally orders us to have fun while we let Him fight the battle for us.

Joshua, in many ways is like us. He's weighed down with the burden of his responsibility, like we all are! We see the things we believe God has called us to do, but we are so prone to running ahead of ourselves and God that we forget to have fun.

Hope you and I can truly look at our "commander" instead of looking at our battles.

Hope you and I can remove our sandals.

    CARRY ON WITH YOUR LIFE, WHILE HE WORKS

16

My English is bad,
but my God is good

Micah 7:8-10, 18-20

Because I try to form a cohesive marriage between each chapter and my current situation, I am going to randomly throw some light on how I am dealing with my professional life right now. And most importantly how that has taught me to rely on God even more.

By now, you've got a fair idea of what my profession has meant to me. I loved being a journalist, loved the commotion inside a newsroom, the deadlines, breaking stories and everything therein. Now after moving to Canada, I've had it pretty tough professionally. I don't intend to get into cross country grievances or how bad and good a certain nation is, but I am simply trying to share all this, in order to draw a co-relation between certain difficult times and God's role in it.

So let's start with my profession. I was a successful journalist in India. And while packing my bags to cross some 11,000 kilometers - I thought restarting my journalism career in Canada - would be a piece of cake. What a delusional fool I was! The piece of cake I got was stale, crusted, tasteless, fungus-filled, smelly and rotten. Hold on before you get all judgy with my euphemisms... Most people who dream of a Canadian passport have had it pretty rough in India. They've either been in wrong professions, harassed by traffic, pollution, poverty, corruption and what not. Unfortunately, India was a breeding ground of goodness for me. My mojo was at its best. The only reason I moved was for love and marriage.

Cut to the present. Once here, I was determined to not fall into the endless rut of "survival jobs" that most new immigrants end up doing. And so I decided to get a post graduate degree to be at par with the Canadian market. After this, a set of brand new challenges awaited me. The bait doubled because journalism is such a niche profession and the Canadians were not going to integrate a brown immigrant woman so easily into a mainstream profession unless I was a born Canadian, or belonged to one of the first world countries (sorry... You and I would love to think of India as the world's sixth biggest economy, fact is, India's image has still not grown beyond Bollywood and spicy cuisine. Oh yeah, and snake charming and free to roam elephants, monkeys and cows!)

     MY ENGLISH IS BAD, BUT MY GOD IS GOOD

So I was told my English is not good. I have zero experience (mind you, my 10 years of journalism experience in India hardly mattered). Some went to extent of saying that I have a raw potential but journalism is not what I should aim for, at least not in Canada!

All my dreams came crashing down piece by piece. I began to self-doubt. Was this THE end? Was my journey over? Was I meant to spend the rest of my Canadian life counting coins at Walmart? IS THIS REALLY TRULY OVER?

In my utter hopelessness and despair, I decided to have a meeting with God. I wanted to ask Him what's going on… is this how He wanted my life to end? Is this how He wanted me to waste my talents, my skills? It was a fruitful meeting, I tell ya. He gave me *Micah 7: 8-10, 18-20*. My answers stared at me right in the face through these verses. And since I love match-the-following (remember school days?), I am going to let you match the answers with each question that I asked above.

8 Do not gloat over me, my enemy!
Though I have fallen, I will rise.
Though I sit in darkness,
the Lord will be my light.

9 Because I have sinned against him,
I will bear the Lord's wrath,
until he pleads my case
and upholds my cause.

He will bring me out into the light;
I will see his righteousness.

10 Then my enemy will see it
and will be covered with shame,
she who said to me,
"Where is the Lord your God?"
My eyes will see her downfall;
even now she will be trampled underfoot
like mire in the streets.

Need I say more? Anything I say after this point will be like putting plastic earrings on your fiancée after giving her a diamond ring.

After my successful time spent with God, I still don't know where and how and when I will restart doing what I love. Which country and city I'll end up living in or where my dreams would eventually take me. But I do know who's in charge. I am of a certain crazy belief that it's His and my joint venture and we'll make it through together.

I might have no Canadian experience but my skillsets are enough for Christ to love me. And you see, my English might be bad, but He's good to me.

17

You silver fox!

Isaiah 46:4-13

Today for the first time, I am not going to put ME in the chapter. And since this book is all about the daily happenings in my current life and how it could possibly serve as a motivational manual to my readers – I have decided to dedicate this chapter to a very special woman in my life – my grandmother.

I lovingly called her *ajji* (Marathi for grandma) and her life was a blazing testimony of what childlike, stubborn, shameless faith in Christ looks like.

She converted to Christianity after marrying my grandfather (who belonged to an aristocratic lineage). Since then this woman who came from a radical Hindu background, endorsed Christianity as if there was no tomorrow. Whether this was an attempt to find acceptance in *abba's* (granddad) home with his high-browed family members or a way to erase her abusive childhood – I don't know! I do however know that she was a bit of a zealot. We collectively shut her up when she mouthed some "insanity" like, "I want to dance for Jesus today." "I am going to make this meal for Jesus, He's gonna dine with us tonight!" or better still, "I am going to sit in Jesus' lap as He puts me to bed." Now don't go all mushy on this. All this sounds kinda cute and puppyish right now, but when we were younger and more conscious of our faith, these statements sounded bizarre, ridiculous and completely schizophrenic! But *ajji* continued to embarrass us and we continued to stop her relentlessly.

She was a fiery woman. Oh yeah, she was. She picked up fights easily. Got mad at almost anyone and everyone. And in her church she came to be known as someone you surely didn't wanna mess around with. But there were three quintessential things in her life, she wouldn't trade off for anyone or anything: Spend at least a couple hours reading Bible, go to church every Sunday, continue to talk about Jesus like you'd brag about your fancy new car or cuddly li'l pet.

In her later years, and esp after *abba* passed away, her dementia kicked in pretty bad. She'd slowly started forgetting things. But up until recently her memory remained enough intact to catch a freakin' bus to the church and even manage her way back home. When her brain finally decided to call it quits – the floodlights were all turned off – almost all of a sudden. She forgot to eat, couldn't tell the difference between

                    YOU SILVER FOX!

raw and cooked food, didn't know a pot was meant for poop and the final shot was when she failed to recognize her own daughter (my mother) who was quite the piece of her heart.

Now imagine caring for such people. It's like looking after a child with special needs. Only in this case, it was a fully developed adult who was 5'10" tall and weighed close to 80 kilos.

Hold that thought right there.

Open your Bibles and read *Isaiah 46: 4* aloud. Yes aloud.

Did you? Come on now...

What does it say? "Even to your old age and gray hairs I am he, I am he who will sustain you. I have made you and I will carry you; I will sustain you and I will rescue you."

Why this particular verse stands out poignantly is because till *ajji's* last breath she was looked after by my mother. In fact *ajji* even passed away in mom's arms. Refusal to put *ajji* at a nursing home and micromanaging her activities, right from the time she woke up to pooped, sat upright or went to bed was managed so meticulously by team mother and house helps that it almost felt like a mission on their part to keep her alive and kicking – albeit – she'd forgotten she had limbs called legs!

So now you know the point I am trying to drive home?

1. It doesn't matter how many fights you picked up or shoulders you scuffed on the way, when you accept Christ as your ultimate savior and lean on Him a bit

crazily and also zealously (I can't believe I am actually saying that!) He takes care of your dark sides as well. Well, self-awareness, willingness to let go etc etc are several other factors in one's growth, but we'll leave that for another time.

2. When you cling on to every word from the Bible as if your life depended on it, He doesn't fail you. Look at how team mother et al looked after *ajji*. And trust me that job was hard. There were days when my mom's finger nails only smelled of feces (from cleaning up potty accidents). And I'll back that up with *Verse 10* that clearly says, "I make known the end from the beginning, from ancient times, what is still to come. I say, 'My purpose will stand, and I will do all that I please.'"

So this non-filter-crazy follower of Christ did get her way in the end. And how? The same church goers who were afraid to rub *ajji* the wrong way, were the first ones present at her funeral.

She's not alive today and as I reminiscence my childhood with her, this is the best parting gift I could give her – her testimony – to others.

I wish I could touch your tender skin one last time,
Look into your deep set eyes, so sublime.
I remember how you always told me that I wasn't born to you, but you were still my mother,
Would I have it any other way rather?

                    YOU SILVER FOX!

No. Because my childhood began with you, and now with your going away I suddenly feel a bit older,

Is this how you planned for my world to be a bit bolder?

So let me say goodbye to you for one last time,

You were crazy, you were brave, you loved God fearlessly and that is the last memory you left at your grave.

Until we again embrace,

And one day soon I'll see your smiling face.

18

Wrongly caught up

2 Samuel 22:26-37

Human lives are funny. We often don't love ourselves enough, then how can we love someone else? We often don't have our own lives straightened out, then how can we raise questions about the inadequacies of someone else's? This is a reality and yet we all succumb to these traps over and over again.

Curiosity, inquisitiveness, gossip, bitching, back biting – does get the better of most of us – point is, are our own lives picture perfect to not be a subject to any of these vices, mentioned above.

The reason I am talking about all this today is because, simply because the world and especially WE as Christians need to know that Christianity is not about being a Bible nerd, knowing each and every verse or mouthing Hallelujah prayers. Honestly, all this is good. And I endorse it very much. But like I've mentioned in my previous chapters, Christianity is more. Much more.

Here's a peek into my personal life. A life that's been pretty adventurous. Yes. I've had a life with exceptional highs and bottomless lows. Every phase of my life has been riddled with challenges, struggles, successes, ecstasy, drama, upturns and downturns. The only difference is that in my past, I'd no one to endorse this craziness. Now, however, I've someone who loves me and accepts me for what I am, who I am, and the way I am or where I am. People have often expressed "concern" by asking my family members questions about my personal life and while I want to tell them that it's none of their business, I now seek my utmost comfort in knowing that "He has kept me from being captured, and I have never fallen." (*2 Samuel 22:37*).

Often when you struggle with existential questions like who am I? Where am I going? How am I going to get there and what will it take for all the suffering to pass? Remember just one thing: "With your help I can advance against a troop, with my God I can scale a wall." (*2 Samuel 22: 30*). For our reference, let's take David for instance. God delivered David from Goliath. Then God delivered David from Saul. The same God delivered him from Israel's enemies, from Absalom and from his own sinful passions.

These verses are so self-explanatory that it needs for no further explanation. Anything done here in excess would be a hyperbole.

All I can say is that taste and see that the Lord is good. I have personally soaked in the goodness of His love and grace and His very presence, ever since I started walking a personal walk with Christ. Yes, it's true. You need to stretch out your hand and hold on to the outstretched arm. If He didn't fail David, despite this man's many a shortcomings, He won't fail you either.

Like David relished the place of victory he had in the Lord and was never hesitant to proclaim it – the best gift we can give our savior, our father, our friend – is the gift to praise Him freely and generously. Often people mistake praise with "buttering" God, and as juvenile as it may sound, a lot of people do that, "Lord, if you give us a car, we'll give you half of our salary… Lord if you give me that job, I'll wash down all the church benches…"

God doesn't want THIS. What He truly wants is your heart. And when that heart slowly starts becoming a reflection of what you always wanted it to be, go out and tell the world how that happened.

This is what I am trying to do here.

                    WRONGLY CAUGHT UP

19

Suffering is good

2 Thessalonians 1:3-12

It's only just a coincidence that as I sit and write my last chapter, there is lightning and thunder outside. It's so Bollywood style filmy, down to the T, but I don't mind this special backdrop. I could even break into a Bollywood dance right now, but I have my final chapter to complete…

So back to real world. The reason I chose these verses is befitting for an awesome conclusion. A conclusion that is almost prayer-like in nature and that sums up why I even started writing this book in the first place.

The way I would interpret this chapter is that it's quite ideal in its outlook. So ideally "we must thank God at all times… It is right for us to do so…" (*Verse 3*) *only a few lines from this verse have been used for the sake of reference.

The actual verse is, "We ought to thank God always for you, brothers and sisters, and rightly so, because your faith flourishes more and more and the love of each one of you all for one another is ever greater."

Almost all the other verses talk about Christ's coming and how He will "ideally" deliver us through suffering… not FROM our suffering but THROUGH our suffering.

We go back to *Verse 3* that begins with Apostle Paul thanking God for what had miraculously taken place in the hearts and lives of these believers (people of the church in Thessalonica). Paul finds himself morally indebted to God for his grace. *Verse 4* further says, "As a result we ourselves boast about you in the churches of God for your perseverance and faith in all the persecutions and afflictions you are enduring."

Now the reason I might have over explained this is because I HATE SUFFERING – like any normal human – but my level of tolerance towards pain is in minus. But as God is God, He's is a master creator at constructing beauty from ashes. Had I not endured the pain of isolation, cultural shock, unemployment, lack of identity in Canada, I'd have never known the glorious ways in which God works. I'd have grown but only in flesh, my soul would be as old as my five-year-old. But today my soul is maturing and I have no one to thank but God! The words, "because your faith flourishes more and more and the love of each one of you all for one another is ever greater," resonates so well with me and my life. And that becomes the focal point of my thanksgiving.

Another interesting observation this chapter offers is that seeking revenge on whoever might have caused you pain is pointless. Why? Because, "It is right for God to repay with affliction those who afflict you." (*Verse 5*)

I have never really been vindictive or revengeful in my heart towards anyone but I wouldn't deny that a part of me hurts when I see those that have caused me pain, flourish! And then I had a beautiful realization one day. If I am focusing on someone's "ideal" and "happy" life and feeling bad because according to me they don't "deserve" it, then where am I seeking the cover of God's grace upon me? What I am seeking or wishing for is someone's unhappiness while, almost in a moment of epiphany I realized that what I really need to look out for is God's grace. I don't need you to be miserable, I just need to look out for what best suits me – GRACE (my favourite word in the Bible).

So He really has your back. He's got you covered.

Through every situation relax and trust Him. And this I can say confidently today because of what I experienced.

In Conclusion…

They say life is twisted, as it always will be. Much to my chagrin, there are no definite blacks and white. There are greys and semi greys and quasi greys and now there are even 50 shades of greys!

But in the midst of these twists and turns when life takes its shape, some come out battered, beaten and bruised. Many a times that has been my state of affairs too. I have felt like giving up, beating my head against the wall or laying down and pretending that I did not exist.

A part of me wants this conclusion to be a bit of an emotional farewell, but that's not coming naturally to me. In fact I am happy and some strange peace flows through me. A peace that indeed passes all understanding.

This journey has been so tumultuous and a very special one too – this whole process of knowing Jesus – on a personal level. And I really don't think I can do without

Him. In silent prayers I often tell Him rather sternly, "You leave me, I die okay!"

I am aware that life will continue to toss unexpected turns which will once again threaten to suck us down. Through these patches that literally "suck" big time, I will give you my own little trick: Harder the time, harder the cling. Hold on to Jesus so tight as if your life and death depended upon that grip. Seen a man hanging on to a rope in the midst of a raging river? That's the hanging I am talking about!

I hope this book can help you and provide any little guidance if any, in your daily walk with Jesus.

I wish you all rainbows and unicorns, but most importantly, I wish you all Christ and His grace.